THE FRANDIDATE

READ ALL OF FRANNY'S ADVENTURES

Lunch Walks Among Us
Attack of the 50-ft. Cupid
The Invisible Fran
The Fran That Time Forgot
Frantastic Voyage
The Fran with Four Brains
The Frandidate

Franny K. Stein

MAD SCIENTIST

THE FRANDIDATE

JIM BENTON

SIMON & SCHUSTER BOOKS FOR YOUNG READERS

NEW YORK LONDON TORONTO SYDNEY

SIMON & SCHUSTER BOOKS FOR YOUNG READERS

An imprint of Simon & Schuster Children's Publishing Division
1230 Avenue of the Americas, New York, New York 10020

First Simon & Schuster Books for Young Readers paperback edition September 2009
Copyright © 2008 by Jim Benton

For information about special discounts for bulk purchases, please contact Simon & Schuster Special Sales at 1-866-506-1949 or business@simonandschuster.com.
The Simon & Schuster Speakers Bureau can bring authors to your live event.
For more information or to book an event, contact the Simon & Schuster Speakers Bureau at 1-866-248-3049 or visit our website at www.simonspeakers.com.
The text for this book is set in Captain Kidd.
The illustrations for this book are rendered in pen, ink, and watercolor.
Manufactured in the United States of America
Also available in a Simon & Schuster Books for Young Readers hardcover edition.
4 6 8 10 9 7 5 3
The Library of Congress has cataloged the hardcover edition as follows:
Benton, Jim.
The Frandidate / Jim Benton.—1st ed.
p. cm.
Summary: Determined to be elected class president, mad scientist Franny K. Stein uses her Atomic Combiner to make a suit that makes her seem to be whatever a voter wants her to be, but the suit has plans of its own.
1. Science—Experiments—Fiction. 2. Politics, Practical—Fiction.
3. Elections—Fiction. 4. Schools—Fiction.
5. Humorous stories.   I. Title.
PZ7.B447547Frd 2008
Fic—dc22
2007050721
ISBN 978-1-4169-0233-1 (hc)
ISBN 978-1-4169-0234-8 (pb)
ISBN 978-1-4169-9664-4 (eBook)
0410 OFF

Dedicated to Pete Hart

ACKNOWLEDGMENTS

Editors: Kevin Lewis and Julia Maguire

Designer: Tom Daly

Art Directors: Laurent Linn and Lizzy Bromley

Production Editor: Katrina Groover

Managing Editor: Jen Strada

Production Manager: Michelle Kratz

CONTENTS

Franny K. Stein
MAD SCIENTIST

THE FRANDIDATE

Chapter One

FRANNY'S HOUSE

The Stein family lived in the pretty pink house with lovely purple shutters down at the end of Daffodil Street. Everything about the house was bright and cheery. Everything, that is, except the upstairs bedroom with the tiny round window.

Behind this window was Franny's room, which was also her laboratory — her Mad Scientist Laboratory.

Franny wasn't your average mad scientist. Franny wasn't planning to take over the universe, or galaxy, or even the world.

Franny thought that maybe she should want to take over the world, being a mad scientist and everything, but it seemed wrong to her somehow.

It was tempting, of course. If she were in charge, she knew she could use her genius to do all sorts of great things that people wouldn't let her do now.

Like, if she added a pinch of kangaroo DNA to human cells, we wouldn't need cars anymore.

And if she made everybody's whole
kitchen a microwave oven, they could just
set the table, press a button, and everything
would cook all at once.

Or she could go ahead with her plan to just
squirt the sunscreen directly on the sun itself,
so we wouldn't have to wipe it on ourselves
all the time.

And if she ever decided to take over the world, she knew nobody would be able to keep her from doing it.

She could have used her Chimpofier to turn everybody into monkeys that she could easily control with a few bananas.

Or she could have simply used her Steiny
Heiny Ray to make everybody's butts so
big they couldn't get out of their chairs to
stop her.

And it would have been easy as pie to just turn everybody into a pie, which often made Franny wonder what she was thinking when she invented a machine that could turn people into pie.

She supposed it was probably something she had made for her lab assistant, Igor. She was always making things like that for him.

Igor was a great lab assistant. Of course, he wasn't a *pure* Lab. He was also part poodle, part Chihuahua, part beagle, part spaniel, part shepherd, and possibly part some kind of weasly thing that probably wasn't even a dog.

Whatever Igor was, he really liked pie, and whatever kind of mad scientist Franny was, she wasn't the type that would take over the world. Not by force. That would be wrong.

CHAPTER TWO
OUCHY COUCHY

Franny was getting ready for school, and Igor was nowhere to be found.

Franny didn't really need Igor's help to get ready, but it was a good idea to keep track of what he was up to.

She peeked around the corner and saw him watching his favorite show, *Miss Wizzywozzle's Story Time.*

"Igor!" she yelled. "Just what do you think you're doing? You know I hate this show. And I think you'll be happier if you hate it too!"

Franny grabbed the remote and pointed it at the TV.

Igor flew through the air and grabbed
Franny's arms, wrestling desperately to keep
her from pointing the device at the TV.

"Let go!" she yelled, and as they grappled
for control, Franny pressed a button on the
remote.

A hot red beam shot from the device and blew a huge smoking hole in the couch, and right through the wall behind it. For a moment, the two of them stared silently at the smoldering sofa.

"That wasn't the TV remote was it?" she asked quietly.

Igor shook his head.

"I shouldn't leave things like this lying around."

"My couch!" Mom yelled as she ran into the room. "My favorite couch! That couch went with everything. Do you know how hard it is to find a couch that goes with everything?"

She looked angrily at Franny and Igor.

"Who did this?"

Franny's brilliant mind had already formulated a flawless explanation that would prove it was all Igor's fault.

Igor knew he would probably get blamed for this and he just closed his eyes and prayed.

Franny's mom stood quietly, staring at
Franny. Franny began to open her mouth to
pin the whole thing on Igor, but when she
looked into her mom's wide, honest eyes,
she couldn't do it. She knew what her mom
wanted.

"It's all my fault, Mom," Franny admitted.

"Thank you for telling the truth, Franny. That's what I wanted. You'll still have to figure out a way to replace this couch, but since you told me the truth, I won't punish you."

Franny's mom plucked the blaster from Franny's hand.

"And let's not leave things like this lying around, okay?"

Franny nodded.

"Now, get your stuff and go to school."

CHAPTER THREE

LET'S GET THIS PARTY STARTED

Miss Shelly was Franny's favorite teacher of all time.

Franny's earlier teachers hadn't really understood her, and it's difficult to learn from somebody that runs screaming from the classroom every time you walk in.

But Miss Shelly was almost never afraid of Franny, and usually had something interesting to teach.

Franny paid close attention as Miss Shelly began writing that day's lesson on the blackboard.

For a moment, Franny was so thrilled that she almost shouted. It looked like Miss Shelly was writing "electricity."

Along with chemistry, nuclear power, and brain removal, electric power was one of Franny's favorite subjects.

But as Miss Shelly finished writing, Franny could see that she had written "election," which, when compared to electricity, sounded pretty darned boring.

"An election is when people vote for a person who will represent them, and organize them, and if necessary, lead them," Miss Shelly explained. "We'll be electing a president of the class."

Franny perked up a little.

"Can this president tell everybody what to do and punish them if they disobey?" Franny asked, while she quickly sketched out a few ideas for a dungeon she could build at the school for just that purpose.

"Well, maybe not punish. But the president can help determine some of the rules in the class, and the president is a person that people usually look up to, and I suppose that the president does tell people what to do," said Miss Shelly.

Franny smiled. Maybe this wasn't so boring.

"So I want you all to decide who you want to be president of the class," Miss Shelly continued. "People who want to be elected are called candidates. If you want to be a candidate for president, you'll need to tell us all why. The class will be sharing these ideas all week long. May the best man win."

Franny smiled to herself. It was more like may the best Fran win.

CHAPTER FOUR

SOME PEOPLE WOULDN'T KNOW A GOOD IDEA IF IT CRAMMED A CARROT DOWN THEIR THROATS

Franny loved the idea of being president. It was kind of like taking over, but if people voted for you, they were *giving* you control. You weren't really taking anything.

The next day Franny came to school with some posters illustrating the improvements she was going to make.

Her ideas were so brilliant that she was
sure as soon as the kids heard them, they
would elect her president on the spot.

BRAIN
ENLARGING
RAY FOR KIDS
THAT AREN'T
SMART ENOUGH

BIG BOTTLES
TO STUFF
NOISY KIDS
IN.

ROBOTS THAT
WILL MAKE
SURE YOU
EAT A
HEALTHY
LUNCH
EVERY DAY

2 + 2 = 5

CHALK THAT EXPLODES
IF YOU WRITE THE
WRONG ANSWER

As Franny was explaining how wonderful exploding chalk would be, she began to realize that the kids were not electing her on the spot.

They weren't applauding. They weren't even smiling. And that one kid who hadn't wet his pants for a long time was squirming, as if he might do it again.

Franny was amazed that when Percy started talking about new playground equipment, three of the kids cheered. And when Alexandra talked about less homework, five of the kids applauded.

It was as if Percy and Alexandra knew exactly what to say to get the group excited.

If Franny was going to win this election, she knew that she'd have to give this class what it wanted.

This was going to take more than a few brilliant posters.

Chapter Five

PLEASING ALL
OF THE PEOPLE
ALL OF THE TIME.
SIMPLE ENOUGH.

Franny started preparing to assemble things her classmates liked.

"The girls like kittens," she said. "And the boys seem to enjoy soccer."

"Everybody likes candy," she said, and Igor ran and got two big bags of chocolate bars.

"And I think they like clowns. They like clowns, don't they?" she asked Igor. Igor shrugged his shoulders.

Franny began tossing everything into her Atomic Combiner. (Most mad scientists have one, you know.)

"And puppies, and crayons, and balloons, and cake," she commanded. Igor handed her one after the other.

Franny began to grin. "And now we atomically combine them, and all that's left is to present it to the class."

Franny pressed the button and the air was filled with the unmistakable aroma of kitten molecules fusing with clown atoms.

CHAPTER SIX

EVERYBODY IS RUNNING FOR THE OFFICE

Franny stood up in front of the class.

"As you know, I'm running for the office of president, and now I'd like to present Part Two of my campaign," she announced.

She pulled the tarp off the big hulking clown-thing that Igor was holding on a leash.

"Elect me and this can be yours!"

It was mostly a clown, but parts of its face looked like a kitten. It had soccer balls for eyes, and cake was leaking out of its ears.

"Behold your future!" Franny yelled triumphantly, although nobody could hear her over the sound of the children's shrieks and the wet choking hacks of the clown-thing coughing up a puppy.

Franny's classmates ran for the office, to get the principal.

Igor led the horrible creation out of the classroom, pausing only for a moment to eat some ear-cake.

"Sorry, Miss Shelly," Franny said. "But I combined everything they like. I don't understand."

"Maybe you should try to think of the class as they see themselves: as individual people, and not just as a group," said Miss Shelly. "You have to know where each voter stands on the issues."

Franny wiped some goo off the coughed-up puppy.

"So you're saying I have to be the exact candidate that every single one of them wants me to be? I don't think that's possible."

"Maybe not, Franny, but if you're going
to get elected, it will be because each person
sees you as the best person for him or her."

CHAPTER SEVEN

THE LITTLE SEW AND SEW

Franny walked into her lab. Igor took one look at her and brought her Snookyfangs, her stuffed bat. Franny smiled a bit. Igor always knew what she wanted even before she asked. *Dogs are like that,* she thought.

She sat down on her chair, but jumped right
back up with a squeal when she realized she
had sat on her chameleon.

"I didn't even see him there! Amazing how
he can change to look like whatever he needs
to," she said to herself. She sat back down to
cuddle up to Snookyfangs and have a think.

Her parrot interrupted the quiet with a perfect imitation of Franny's squeal.

Franny didn't like to be mocked, but it was hard not to admire how quickly this bird could make any sort of sound it wanted.

"Quite a talent," Franny said.

Suddenly Franny sprang to her feet, sending Snookyfangs flying.

"That's it!" she howled, and Igor ran for cover. A howling mad scientist can be a very bad thing.

"Sensing what people want, looking any way you need to, sounding like whatever you want to. The answers are here. They're all right here in the lab!"

Franny started activating various machines,
her fantastic mad-scientist brain racing ahead
to the next step, and the one after that.

"Igor! Fetch me my sewing machine!"

CHAPTER EIGHT

MAKING A STRANGE BEDFELLOW

Franny took DNA samples from Igor, the parrot, and the chameleon, and she tossed them into her new improved Atomic Combiner.

These animals had the special abilities to sense feelings, mimic, and change appearance, and Franny wanted those abilities.

Her creation would have to be convincing, so she threw in a little sample from a cobra, for its ability to hypnotize its prey, and a specimen from a spider, for its ability to lure things into its web.

She gave her creation nerves of steel, so it wouldn't get nervous when it spoke in front of people. She added a handful of spicy peppers, to give her creation a fire in its belly.

"A fire in the belly means that it will really want to win," she explained to Igor.

Franny added a dash of python and a scrap of a carpet.

"The python should give it a strong grasp of the issues," she said with a grin, "and the carpet will make it an expert on where people stand."

Franny threw a few switches, and the electricity began to crackle. She pushed a big lever, and the iron rollers turned, uncoiling a strange, floppy piece of fabric onto the floor.

It looked like a big gray bed sheet, but it was warm and soft, like skin. When Franny touched it, it wiggled and twitched.

"I think it likes to be tickled," Franny said, and she dragged the bed sheet over to her sewing machine.

Igor held a pincushion for Franny and watched her cut and sew for hours.

With each stitch, it looked like Franny might be assembling one of her typical monsters, except that this thing had no guts, no spine, and only a very tiny brain.

Finally, it was complete.

"Igor, wait until you get a load of this," she said.

And then Igor got a load of it.

It wasn't really a monster. It was sort of a costume, or maybe it was more like a skin, or a hide.

Franny began slipping it on.

As she stepped into it, she seemed a bit taller right away. And her arms seemed longer.

She pulled up the hood, and stood in front of Igor, modeling her strange baggy suit.

"What do you think?" she said, her voice muffled inside the skin.

Before Igor could respond, the skin began to change shape.

Sensing that Igor found it scary and disgusting, the skin quickly took on the appearance of Miss Wizzywozzle, the host of Igor's favorite TV show.

Igor didn't know what to think. Part of him knew this was Franny, but part of him wanted to believe that Miss Wizzywozzle had come to the house to visit.

"It works!" Franny shouted, although the voice came out sounding just like Miss Wizzywozzle's.

"It can sense exactly what somebody is thinking and feeling, and it becomes whatever they want it to be. It's the perfect candidate.

"I've created THE FRANDIDATE!"

CHAPTER NINE

THE SELF-MADE FRAN

Franny walked into the classroom confidently. She was wearing the Frandidate skin, and since the Frandidate was sensing only what Franny wanted it to be, it looked a lot like Franny, although maybe a little taller, and a little less mad-scientist-y.

Before class started, Franny decided to go around the room and talk to kids one by one. She started with Mary.

The Frandidate immediately sensed that Mary was a little afraid of Franny, and it transformed itself into a bunny wearing a dress. It could tell that Mary liked penguins, too, and so a penguin pattern suddenly emerged on the Frandidate's dress.

Franny listened from inside as the Frandidate sensed other things that were important to Mary.

Franny shared some sort of strange connection with the skin, and she could tell exactly what Mary wanted to hear.

"Vote for Franny, and there will be more time devoted to dolls every day," Franny said through the Frandidate's mouth.

Mary clapped and smiled. Franny made a note to herself that if elected, she'd need to keep that promise.

Franny navigated the Frandidate skin around the room. It grew taller for the kid who liked basketball, and even looked like it was wearing a uniform.

Then it looked like a chef, a grandma, a superhero, and an elf. It changed its voice, its size, and even how it walked, to suit each individual kid.

The skin gave Franny the ability to sense what each kid wanted to hear, and so she talked about the things each kid liked.

And sometimes Franny didn't talk at all. She discovered that the Frandidate could do the talking all by itself. It didn't have a big brain, but this talking didn't seem to require a lot of thought.

Franny just sat back and enjoyed the ride. And after she had finished talking to everybody, Franny took her seat.

"Franny for President! Franny for President!" all the kids chanted. Even the kids who had been running against Franny were cheering for her now.

Miss Shelly didn't know what to think, but there was only one conclusion to make. "Looks like we don't even have to vote. Franny, you win by a landslide."

The words made the Frandidate's skin
tingle, as if it had received a little electric
shock. It liked the feeling, and so did Franny.

As president of the class, she might find
it tricky to keep all the promises she had
made, but Franny was a genius, and she was
confident that she could handle the job.

CHAPTER TEN

FROM THE PINK HOUSE TO THE WHITE ONE

F ranny was delighted. She wore the suit all the way home, and as she saw people, the suit made little changes in itself based on what it sensed they wanted it to be.

When she got home, she looked in the
mirror. The Frandidate skin, sensing Franny's
feelings, wiggled, and wriggled, and changed.

In the mirror, Franny didn't see a little girl
who had won a class election anymore. She
saw a leader, the president of a country: the
President of the United States of America.

The thought made the Frandidate's skin tingle again, like a little more electric power had been run through it, and the sensation made Franny smile.

"Why not?" she said. "Once elected, I can use my genius to do all sorts of great things for people, and if they choose to vote for me, it's not like I'm trying to take over the world or anything. It's their choice."

Franny started to slip out of the Frandidate suit, but the zipper stuck and she couldn't get the suit all the way off.

"I'll fix the zipper later," she said, walking around with the skin halfway off.

"Igor, warm up my Satellite-Snagger," she said, and Igor pointed the device toward the sky.

CHAPTER ELEVEN

ICU, ICU, AND ICU2

Franny had Igor lock on to a television satellite. She knew he could do it, because once Igor had locked himself in the lab and used it to make every TV in the world play *Miss Wizzywozzle's Story Time*. Because he loved the show, he wanted to make everybody else love it too.

Last month Franny had figured out how to get a return picture from other people's TVs. If she wanted to, she could simply type in your name and then watch you through your TV.

She called it the ICU2, and she had quite a few laughs at people walking around in their underpants, but she had never thought of a really good use for it — until now.

Franny revealed her plan to Igor.

"You just keep that satellite locked in position. The cameras will be on me inside the Frandidate skin," she said, pulling the skin on the rest of the way.

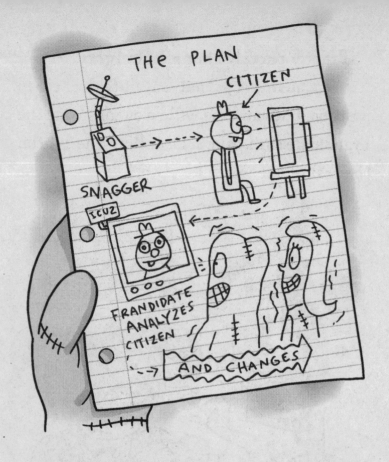

"The system is going to activate every TV in the country, and the ICU2 will send us a picture of the viewer. The Frandidate will sense what each person wants, and it will change its shape according to those feelings. All I'll need to say is something like 'vote Franny K. Stein for president.'"

Igor looked a little uncomfortable. The Frandidate skin helped Franny sense Igor's concerns.

"This is not like taking over the world," said Franny. "If the voters elect me as president, it's because they freely choose to do so. It's not by force. I'm not making them do it. It's *their* choice."

Igor nodded. That made sense.

"And think of all the good I could do if I got elected."

Igor nodded again.

"Now, look at this," she said. "The system will automatically measure the amount of success we're having, so we can look at this Support Meter and know second-by-second just how many voters we have on our side."

Igor looked at the clock.

"Don't worry about the timing. The Frandidate moves fast, and as it does more and more of this, my calculations say that it will get easier and easier for the skin to do its thing."

Igor pointed at a second camera, which was aimed at the Frandidate from a different angle.

"Oh, right. And it's going to do it twice as fast as you might have imagined. Wait until you see this."

The Frandidate skin wriggled and squirmed, and Igor watched a second set of features erupt out of its head.

"See?" Franny said from inside. "We can use both cameras. Isn't it great? It's two-faced!"

CHAPTER TWELVE

I KNOW WHERE YOU STAND. HERE'S WHERE I LIE.

The cameras and monitors hummed. Images of people started popping up and the Frandidate swiftly got impressions of what they wanted and instantly changed its appearance.

From inside, Franny marveled at the Frandidate's skill. It changed to look like a butcher, a baker, a candlestick maker. It became old, it became young. It could look like a man or a woman. It could imitate anything.

Franny could sense what the Frandidate was feeling.

"Vote for Franny K. Stein," Franny said, and it came out in hundreds of accents, dozens of languages, and countless different voices.

And it sounded very persuasive. The Support Meter continued to climb, and the Frandidate's skin tingled more and more as it did.

It really loves the support, Franny thought.

Every few minutes, Igor would get worried and peek up from his satellite controls. When the Frandidate saw that he was looking, it would turn into Miss Wizzywozzle, and Igor felt calm again.

It is nice to have Miss Wizzywozzle in the lab, he thought, even if deep down he knew it wasn't really Miss Wizzywozzle.

"And if elected, I'll make sure that old ladies never get sick," the Frandidate told one old lady.

How am I going to keep that promise? Franny thought.

"I will outlaw brussels sprouts," it said to another person. "And everybody will get their own unicorn."

"Wait a second!" Franny shouted. "I can't promise that," she said, but her voice didn't come out of the Frandidate's mouth. It was ignoring her now, and saying everything for itself.

Franny tried to get the zipper opened, but it had completely disappeared.

"Let me out! Stop the broadcast!" she howled, but her voice couldn't escape the Frandidate skin, and worse: The skin was getting tighter.

CHAPTER THIRTEEN

THE THING THAT WOULD BE KING

Everybody will have everything they want!" the Frandidate exclaimed, waving its fist in the air. "I will put an end to all of those people that don't believe as you do," it snarled.

From inside the skin, Franny was trying her best to break free, but the skin was constricting around her.

"It must be the python DNA," she whispered in a strangled gasp.

The Frandidate's eyes became even more intense.

"King of the World!" it said. "Make me King of the World and all your dreams will come true!"

Franny could still barely see out one of the Frandidate's eyes. The Support Meter indicated that the people watching at home believed the Frandidate. They were going to vote for this horrible creation. They were going to make it King of the World.

Franny was still connected to the Frandidate's mind, and she could even see the plan it was already beginning to form.

It never wanted that tingly feeling to stop. It would say anything for it. It would do anything to stay in control.

The Frandidate could destroy the world.

Franny felt herself beginning to faint. She was getting dizzy and it was hard to breathe. She knew that she wasn't just wearing the Frandidate anymore; she had been swallowed by it. It was almost like she had been eaten.

CHAPTER FOURTEEN

QUICK! WHAT CAN SET YOU FREE?

The Frandidate was making all sorts of claims to get people's support.

"I will protect you from everything," it bellowed. "The bad guys won't be bad anymore."

The Support Meter kept going up and up.

Igor suddenly had a very strong impression that it wasn't Franny who was saying these things.

He looked at the Frandidate and it changed to look like Miss Wizzywozzle again, but it didn't make Igor comfortable anymore.

Igor was sensing something else. Dogs are like that.

Igor knew he had to do something.

He couldn't attack it—Franny was in there. He thought of turning off the camera, but as soon as he did, the Frandidate sensed his thoughts and extended a long tentacle to hold him in his chair while it worked the controls itself.

Suddenly, he thought of the one thing that had saved him before. Maybe, just maybe, it could work again, he hoped, and he acted quickly before the Frandidate could stop him.

Igor hit a few switches on the Satellite-Snagger and the system quickly locked on to a very specific television.

It locked on to the one in the pretty pink house with lovely purple shutters down at the end of Daffodil Street.

The ICU2 displayed Franny's mom on the screen.

The Frandidate looked into her wide, honest eyes, and sensed exactly the one thing she wanted.

The Frandidate twitched and sweated.

Igor hit a few more switches and sent the broadcast to every home in the world.

It started to stammer and stutter. There was no way around this.

"I, uh. I just say whatever I know the viewers want to hear," the Frandidate said softly, casting its eyes down in shame.

Inside, its muscles relaxed enough for Franny to catch her breath. It pulled back the tentacle that was holding Igor.

"The promises I made aren't going to be kept, and I really don't care much about the people that vote for me. Once elected, I'll just do whatever I want," it wheezed.

It began to look more like the stitched-up sack of skin it really was, and the Support Meter started to turn backward.

"I'm hollow inside," it said. "I was put together. I was manufactured."

People all over the world sat in front of their TVs, blinking their eyes, wondering what they had liked about the Frandidate in the first place.

"I'm nothing," it finally admitted.

The truth was what Franny's mom wanted, and that was what the Frandidate had given her.

Igor stopped the broadcast, and Franny burst through the skin, gasping for breath. The truth had saved her. The truth had set her free.

"We should print that on a T-shirt or something," she said as she angrily kicked the floppy Frandidate skin out of the way.

Chapter Fifteen

JUST NOT CUT OUT FOR POLITICS

A few days later, Franny and her mom were sitting at the kitchen table. The front page of the newspaper was all about the new president.

"Sure glad they didn't elect that Frandidate thing I made, huh, Mom?" she said. Franny knew she had almost destroyed the world again and was a little embarrassed about it.

"I'll say," Franny's mom said. "That was a close one."

"You know what's weird, Mom? The Support Meter never fell to zero. There was still one person that didn't totally abandon the Frandidate.

"That one person was me, Franny. After the facts came out, I never would have voted for the awful thing. But in the end, I did admire the fact that at least it told the truth. Anybody who tells the truth can't be all bad."

"I'm glad to hear you say that, Mom," Franny said, smiling.

Franny followed her mom into the family room and asked her to sit down on the couch.

"Hey!" she said. "My new couch! You replaced it!"

It was a perfect pale green with light brown stripes, which was exactly the couch her mom had wanted at that very moment.

The couch had sensed it.

And down at the other end of the couch, Igor was surrounded in a pattern of dog bones and happy little Miss Wizzywozzle faces.

He no longer felt like everybody needed to like what he liked. It was okay if it was just for him.

This truly was a couch that could go with anything.

Franny's mom was happy, and Igor was happy, and the couch could sense it, and it made the couch happy too: much happier than it had been when it had been the Frandidate.

Franny understood that her creation just wasn't cut out to be president.

And somewhere in its tiny brain, the Frandidate realized it too. For the first time since its creation, it was no longer interested in where people stood on the issues.

It was much more interested in where they sat.